Anonymous

The New-Year's gift

Containing the history of Master Tommy Thoroughgood and Master

Tommy Froward

Anonymous

The New-Year's gift

*Containing the history of Master Tommy Thoroughgood and Master Tommy
Froward*

ISBN/EAN: 9783337281687

Printed in Europe, USA, Canada, Australia, Japan

Cover: Foto ©Raphael Reischuk / pixelio.de

More available books at **www.hansebooks.com**

THE
NEW-YEAR's GIFT;

CONTAINING

The HISTORY of
Master TOMMY THOROUGHGOOD,

AND

Master FRANCIS FROWARD,

Two Apprentices to the same Master.

To which is added,

The HISTORY of
Little POLLY MEANWELL,

Who, by being Good, was afterwards

QUEEN OF *PETULA*.

ADORNED with CUTS.

Gainsbrough:
Printed at MOZLEY and CO.'s Lilliputian
Book-Manufactory.—1796.

THE

HISTORY

OF

Master TOMMY THOROUGHGOOD,

AND

Master FRANCIS FROWARD,

Two Apprentices to the same Master.

MASTER *Thomas Thoroughgood,* the younger son of a country gentleman, was put out apprentice to an eminent tradesman in *Cheapside, London.* The master finding his busi-

nefs increafe, was obliged to take ano-
ther about two years after, who name
was *Francis Froward.*

Thomas had behaved exceeding well,
was very diligent and honeſt, as well
as good: he uſed to ſay his prayers
conſtantly every morning and night;
he never went to play when he ſhould
be at church or about his maſter's buſineſs: never was known to tell a lye,

nor never ftaid when he was fent on an errand. Thefe rare qualifications had gained him the affections of his mafter and miftrefs, and made him a favourite in the family before *Francis* came to them. It was in a great meafure owing to mafter *Tommy*'s character in the neighbourhood, that Mr. *Froward* was induced to comply with the mafter's demands, not doubting but his fon, in fuch a happy fituation, and with a companion of fo fweet a difpofition, would one day turn out to his fatisfaction, and be a comfort to him in his old age.

Francis, in the firft year of his apprenticefhip, began to difcover the natural bent of his inclination. He chofe to affociate with naughty boys in the ftreets, and feemed to place his whole delight in loofe and idle diverfions; he neglected the bufinefs of the

shop when **at** home, and entirely forgot
it when he **was** abroad. These, and
many more indiscretions of the like nature, *Tommy Thoroughgood* concealed at
first from his master, though not without
some inward uneasiness.

In the fourth year's service, our
young spark, who was an only child,
and heir to a pretty fortune, gave farther proofs of his vicious turn of mind,

and frequently launched out in folies and debaucheries of a more heinous nature; for now he made no scruple of absenting himself from church on the Lord's day; always staid out late when he knew his master was engaged in company, and at such times very rarely returned home so er; nay, he had sometimes the assurance to lie out of his master's house all night. In order to deter him from pursuing this wicked course of life, Mr. *Throughgood* threatened to inform his master of his scandalous behaviour, and to acquaint his parents of his misconduct. But alas! all these menaces proved ineffectual, and instead of working out his reformation, served only to heighten his resentment, and to raise daily squabbles and animosities between them. Hereupon Mr. *Throughgood* finding all his good offices hitherto

thrown away at length determined
no more to meddle in the affair, or
even to offer his brotherly service; but
to leave the unhappy youth to follow
the dictates of his own perverse will;
being resolved at the same time to
take particular care that he should not,
in any of his mischievous frolics, de-

fraud his master, and therefore cast an odium upon his fellow-apprentice.

The master was chosen alderman of the ward, and Mr. *Thoroughgood* was out of his time in the same year: and

from his faithful service, and unblameable conduct, had now the whole management of the trade, as well broad as at home, committed to his care and inspection. This great charge, oblig ed him to keep a stricter eye over *Francis's* behaviour, who was just entering into the last year of his apprenticeship, and imagined his actions were above the cognizance of one, who, the other day was but his equal; and on this account would neither bear his reproof, nor hearken to his admonition; but continued to riot in all the follies and degeneracies of human nature, till his apprenticeship was expired. So true it is, that *the wicked hath the reproof, but the wise man lendeth his ear to instruction.*

Mr. *Francis* having been for a long while impatient of a servile life, **was** now become his own master, and seemed eager of putting himself upon a level with his late companion. To effect this, he goes down to his father, and prevails upon him to set him up in the business, that he might trade for himself. The reins where no sooner laid on his neck, then he gave a loose to his sensual appetites, and in little more than four years had a statute of bankruptcy taken out against him. The unexpected news of this fatal event instantly broke his mother's heart, nor did the old gentleman survive her long. Hereupon our heir was obliged to sell the personal and mortgage the real estate, to procure his liberty, and to satisfy the assignees. In this sinking situation, after the days of mourning were over, he lett the house his father lived in, and returned again to *London*, where he purchased a handsome equipage, commenced the fine gentleman, frequented the balls, masquerades, play houses, routs, drums,

&c. &c. and cut as good a figure as
the best of them.   But here let us
leave him for a while, and turn our eyes
to a worthier object.

In the same space of time which Mr.
Froward took to squander away a
good estate, Mr, *Thoroughgood* had, by
his own industry, and from a small

fortune, gained one considerably better, and was in a fair way of encreasing it. The former made pleasure his business, but the latter made business his pleasure, and was rewarded accordly. The alderman, who by his own application, and Mr. *Thoroughgood's* assiduity, was grown very rich, had no child now living but a daughter,

of whom both he and his lady were extremely fond; they had nothing so much at heart as to see her well settled in the world. She was the youngest, and just now turned of twenty. She had many suitors, but resolved to encourage none without the consent of her parents, who would often, when by themselves, tell her that it was their joint opinion she could not dispose of herself better than to Mr. *Thomas*, and would frequently ask how she liked him? for they would be unwilling to marry her against her own inclination. Her usual answer was, " Your " choice shall be mine; my duty " shall never be made subservient to " any sensual passion." This reply was not so full and expressive as they expected; and as mothers are commonly very dexterous in finding out their daughters maladies, madam had

a good reason to believe, from some
observations she made on mif-beha-
viour, that her affections were already
fixed, and that she was deeply in love
with somebody else, which was the
cause of her unusual anxiety. Hereupon, as she was fitting at work one
evening in a melancholy posture, they
called her and desired to be informed

A 9

whether the husband they proposed was disagreeable to her, if so, she should chuse for herself.

The young lady (after some hesitation) with blushes confessed her regard for Mr. Thoroughgood; which gave infinite satisfaction to the alderman and his lady, who were overjoyed at the prospect they had of marrying their daughter to a person of such prudence integrity, and honour.

The next day, as soon as dinner was over, the alderman and his lady withdrew, and left the two lovers together all the evening; from this interview they became sensible of each other's approaching happiness, and

A 10

about a month after were joined together, to the great satisfaction of all
parties concerned. From this day the
bridegroom was taken into partner-
ship, and transacted the whole business
himself. In process of time his father-
in-law died, and left him in possession
of all his substance. He succeeded
him also in his dignity, and after hav-

ing ſerved the office of ſheriff, was in a
few years called to the chair.

Mr. Froward, whom we left a while
ago purſuing his pleaſures and wicked
inclinations, had long before this time
been reduced to poverty; and, like
many other thoughtleſs wretches, be-
took himſelf to the highway and ga-
ming-table, in hopes of recovering a
loſt fortune. He had followed this

destructive trade with some success, and, without being discovered, above three years; but at length was taken near *Enfield*, and brought to his trial at the *Old Bailey*, during his fellow-prentice's mayoralty, and cast for life. When he was brought to the bar to receive sentence, his lordship recollecting Mr. Froward s name, examined who he was, and asked if he was not the same person that served his time with Mr. Alderman***, in *Cheapside*. This he positively denied; but notwithstanding himself, his person and speech betrayed him.   My lord, animated with principles of the compassion and benevolence and imagining that his design of concealing himself in his wretched situation might very probably proceed from shame or despair, took no farther notice of it in court,

but, forgetting his prefent difgrace, as
well as his former arrogance, and difcre-
tion, privately procured his fentenpe
to be changed into tranfportation for
life.

The fhip in which Mr. Froward
embarked, by ftrefs of weather drove
into a certain port in *Jamaica*, where

he, in less than ten days, was sold to
a noted planter, and doomed to per-
petual slavery. You may imagine
how shocking this prospect must ap-
pear to a gentlemen, who had just before squandered away a good estate in
indolence and pleasure, who never
knew what it was to work, nor had
ever given himself time to think upon
the nature of industry. However, he
no sooner began to reflect upon his

present wretched situation, and his
late providential deliverance from
death, than he also began to repent
of his former transgressions; and finding himself in a strange country, un-
known to any person about him, he
patienttly submitted his neck to the
yoke, and endured his servility with
an uncommon fortitude of mind. In
the first place, he determined, during

all the time of his labour, to offer up
continual thankſgiving to Almighty
God for his manifold mercies beſtowed
on ſo unworthy a creature, and to de-
vote all his leiſure hours to the duty of
repentance. His next reſolution was
to obey his maſter's commands, to
obey him faithfully, and to perform
whatever buſineſs was impoſed on him,
ſo far and ſo long as his health and
ſtrength would permit; not doubting
but the ſame God, who had preſerved
him hitherto, in ſuch a wonderful
manner would accept the oblations
of a contrite heart, and enable him to
go through it with courage and chear-
fulneſs.

The firſt month's ſervice, as he himſelf told me, went very hard with him.
His hands bliſtered, his feet grew
ſore and raw, and the heat of the cli-

mate was almoſt inſupportable; but,
as cuſtom makes every ſtation familiar,
before three months were expired, all
theſe grievances were at an end; and
he, naturally endowed with a ſpirit of
emulation, would not ſuffer himſelf
to be outdone by any of his fellow
ſlaves. The ſuperintendant obſerving
his extraordinary aſſiduity, could not
help taking notice of him, and would
frequently give him encouragement,

either by calling him off to go on a trivial errand, or by thrusting some money in his hand. He behaved in this manner near two years, when his master was informed of his good disposition, and removed him from that laborious employment to an easier, where he had more frequent opportunities of paying adoration to that Almighty Being, who supported him under all his afflictions. In these intervals, he was generally found with a book in his hand, or on his knees, from which practice he received great consolation, as he often assured me.

At the expiration of three years, Sir Thomas Thorougood, who made previous enquiry after his fellow-prentice's behaviour abroad, sent orders to his agent in *Jamaica*, to purchase Mr. Froward's freedom, and to advance him 100*l.* that he might be enabled to get his own livelihood; but

at the same time gave strict orders to
his friend, not to let Mr. Froward
know who was his benefactor, and to
lay his master under the same injunc-
tion. In a short time after Mr. Froward was discharged from slavery; but
did not express so much joy on the
occasion, as might have been reason-
ably expected. From the good usage
he met with in servitude, and the unusual favours he received from the su-
perintendant, as well as the planter,
he had conceived a great liking for
the latter, and seemed to part with
him not without some inward reluc-
tance, though with apparent surprise;
which was much heightened by the
additional favour of a note for a hundred pounds payable upon sight to Mr.
Francis Froward or order, delivered
to him by the same hand, soon after
he received the discharge before men-

tioned. During this confusion, the
gentleman, who really had **a** value
for his late servant, told him he was
welcome to be at his house till he was
settled, and that he would do all the
good offices in his power, to promote
his future welfare. Mr. Froward re-
plied, " Sir, you cannot do me greater
" service than to let me know who is
" my generous benefactor; because
" it is incumbent upon me to make

" fome acknowledgment." The mafter pofitively refufed to do this, and
turned off the difcourfe, by afking
how he intended to difpofe of himfelf
and money. " Sir, (fays he, I am
" not unacquainted with the nature
" of trade, and labour is now become
" habitual to me, and as I am well
" fkilled in the cultivation of the fu-
" gar cane, I would willingly rent a
" fmall plantation of that kind, and
" work upon it for myfelf." The
planter approved of this defign, and pro-
mifed him affiftance.

In about a month after, Mr. Froward met with a bargain, agreeable to
his fubftance, and worked upon it as
hard as if he had been a real flave,
with this difference only, that he could
now fpare more time in the fervice of
his all powerful Redeemer. In the
interim, his late matter procured him

a wife, with a handsome fortune, who
had a sugar-work of her own, and
some negroes; he purchased more,
and, by his industry, thrived a main,
and in a few years laid up 100*l.* in
specie.

In this comfortable state, nothing
gave him uneasiness, but that he could
not come to the knowledge of his kind
benefactor; never was man more anx-

ious to shew his gratitude, or more fo-
licitous to find out his friend! One
day as he was at his devotions, a
strange gentleman came to his habita-

tion, and desired to see him. He was
no sooner admitted, than he accosted
him in the following manner: " Mr.
" *Froward*, I am commander of the
" *Dove* frigate, whose principal own-

" er is Sir *Tho. Thouroughgood*, and am
" juſt arrived from *England* : By Si:
" *Thomas*'s orders I am to inform you
" that his *Jamaica* agent is dead, and
" he has made choice of you to ſuc-
" ceed him here in that ſtation. I have
" a commiſſion from him, for you, in
" my pocket to diſpoſe of my cargo,
" and to freight me again for my voy-
" age home. He never would own it,
" but I am well aſſured, he is the per-
" ſon who ſaved your life, who re-
" deemed you from bondage, and was
" the ſole inſtrument of your preſent
" proſperity." Nothing could have
given Mr. Froward ſo great pleaſure
and ſatisfaction, as this laſt piece of
intelligence; he knew not how to
make the captain welcome enough, he

kept him all night, and in the morning
made him a present of a hogshead of
rum. He made all the possib'e dispatch
in disposing of his cargo, and freighted
him out with the utmost expedition.
With the rest of the goods, he sent Sir
Thomas ten hogsheads of sugar, and as
many of rum, for a present, with the
following letter.

" Honoured Sir,

Tranſported with joy, and drowned
in tears, I ſend this teſtimony of my
eſteem, of which I humbly hope your
acceptance, as well as of thoſe ſmall
tokens of my gratitude with which it
is accompanied.   Next under God,
'tis to you, dear Sir, that I owe, my
life, my liberty, and my all. Happy
me, had I liſtened to your advice in
my nonage! happy ſtill, as by your
means, I have been directed to the
paths of virtue.   'Tis to you I am
indebted for my preſent comfortable
ſituation and the dawning proſpect of
future happineſs; the bills of lading,
&c. are ſent by Mr. ***, and all your
buſineſs here, with which I am en-
truſted, ſhall be executed with the
utmoſt diligence and fidelity. I have
only to add my prayers for the conti-

huation of your life and health, who
have been fo beneficial to many, but
more particularly to, Honoured Sir,

your moft unworthy fervant,

FRANCIS FROWARD."

Sir Thomas was highly pleafed with
the purport of his letter, though he ral-
lied the captain for letting him know' to
whom he was obliged for his freedom.
The fame fhip was fent the next feafon
on the fame voyage, when the captain
was ordered to pay Mr. Froward the full
price for the rum and fugar he had fent
to the knight, and to deliver him the
following letter.

Mr. FROWARD,

" Sir,

I thank you for the acknowledgment
you made for the good offices I did you,
and shall ever esteem the present as it was
intended ; but have neither power nor
inclination to rob you of any thing you
have acquired by dint of merit. My design
is, to add to your acquisitions, and not
to diminish them, as you will experience :
only persevere in your present course of
life, and you will make me ample amends
for all I have, or can do for you.

I am, Sir, your real friend,

T. THOROUGHGOOD."

Mr. Froward, who was uneasy that his friend refused his present, continued in a thriving condition several years. And now his wife died without issue; he, grown very rich, and advanced in years, disposed of the sugar-work, and left off all manner of business, except that of Sir Thomas Thoroughgood's. At length he himself

was feized with a peftilential fever, and carried off in a few days. He bore the the torture of his diftemper with exemplary patience, and met his approaching deftiny with an intrepidity of foul fcarce to be parallelled. That you may the better judge of his fentiments of gratitude, I have herewith fent a copy of his laft will.

In the name of God, Amen. I *Francis Froward* of——, in *Jamaica*, being found in mind and memory, do hereby make my laft will and teftament, in form and manner following, that is to fay;

Imprimis, I bequeath my foul to Almighty God that gave it, hoping, and full trufting, that I fhall be faved and made eternally happy by the mérits of my dear Redeemer *Jefus*

Christ, who suffered for me and all mankind.

Item. As the poor convicts in prison, where I had once the misfortune to be confined, are not attended and instructed as they ought to be, by persons who seek their eternal salvation; I do give and bequeath fifty pounds a year, to purchase for their use such books as the archbishop of *Canterbury*, the bishop of *London*, and the sheriffs of *London* and *Middlesex* shall think proper to put into their hands.

Item. As the laws of *England*, however wisely constructed, have made no provision for poor people born in distant parts, and become miserable there, but left them to perish in the streets, lanes, and public places; I do give and bequeath five hundred pounds a year, to be laid out for their relief, in such a manner as shall seem most agreeable to the lord mayor of *London*, for the time being

and to the truftees that fhall be nomina-
ted by my executors.

Item. And as many poor tradefmen
and labourers are artfully feduced and
perfuaded to enter themfelves on board
merchant-fhips for this and other colonies in his majefty's dominions : and are
afterwards at fea unwarily drawn in to
indent themfelves fervants to the owners
of the veffel, and from that moment
commence flaves, and as fuch are fold in
the public markets of the colonies, and
generally ill-treated ; I do give and bequeath five hundred pounds a year for the
redemption of fuch unhappy people and
for the profecution of thofe who have been
the abettors and contrivers of their ruin.

Item. As gratitude is of all oblations
the greateft and moft acceptable, I do
give and bequeath to my dear friend Mr.
Thomas Thoroughgood, merchant in *London*, who faved me from an ignominious

death and redeemed me from flavery, all the reft and refidue of my real and perfonal eftate; and I do nominate and appoint him, and his heirs and executors, my heirs and executors for ever. In witnefs whereof I have hereunto fet my hand and feal, this thirdday of *May*, 1680.

Witnefs,   FRANCIS FROWARD.

Thomas Williams,
John Wilfon,
Richard Jones.

THE

HISTORY

OF LITTLE

POLLY MEANWELL,

Who was afterwards the

QUEEN of *PETULA*.

POLLY MEANWELL's father and mother died when she was very young, and left her to the care of an uncle, who was an old rich batchelor, covetous to the last degree, and one who cared for nobody but himself. He put her to school a little after her parents death, but finding that by a flaw in some writings, he had the power of taking every thing to himself, he did so, and deprived poor *Polly* of what her father and mother left for her subsistence, and turned her out of doors.

Polly was at first very uneafy at lo-
fing all her fine cloaths, and at being
obliged to go to hard work, which
Mr. *Williams*, the parfon of the pa-
rifh, obferving, that good man came
to her one day, and comforted her in
this manner.   " Don't be caft down,
" *Polly*, at your fine cloaths being
" gone, thofe ragged ones will keep
" you warm, and that is the only ufe
" of cloaths; for people are not a bit
" the better for wearing fine garments.
" 'Tis true, you can't have your tea
" and your coffee, your tarts and your
" cheefecakes, your cuftards and fyl-
" labubs as ufual, but what does that
" fignify ? You can by your labour
" get other victuals : then your work-
" ing for it makes it go down the
" fweeter, and at the fame time keeps
" you in health ; the bed you lie up-
" on feems as foft, after a hard day's

" work, as your down beds, I suppose
" used to be; why then should you
" be uneasy? Be a good girl, say
" your prayers, and put your trust in
" God Almighty; and he will give
" you what his all-knowing wisdom
" sees you want.' *Polly* was so plea-
sed with this speech, that she dropt
Mr. *Williams* a courtesy, and, for the
future, resolved to mind nothing but
her duty, and not repine at Providence.

As she went to church constantly,
and was very devout there, every body took notice of her, and one merchant's wife in particular, sent to the
sexton to know what little ragged girl
that was that came to church constantly, and behaved so well there. The
sexton answered, that 'twas *Polly*
Maxwell; and, " Madam," said he,
" though *Polly* is so poor and so rag-

" ged, she is the best girl in the pa-
" rish." " Is she so?' says the lady,
" then pray give her this new bible;
" and this piece of money;" and put
into his hand a crown for her. Some
time afterwards, this lady, who was
very rich, dropped, as she was step-
ping into her coach, a green purse full
of guineas, and a fine diamond ring,
which *Polly* had the good fortune to
pick up. Now some naughty girls

would have kept all this money, and not have carried it to the lady; and indeed one of her neighbours advised her to do so. But *Polly* was angry with

her, and told her, she was a wicked woman to put such naughty things into a little girl's head. "How can I

" go to church and say my prayers to
" God Almighty, says she, and at the
" same time be guilty of such a dif-
" honeft thing? and what good do you
" think this money will do me? why

" none; 'twill only corrupt what lit-
" tle I get by my labour, and make
" God Almighty angry with." So
fhe got a paper wrote, and nailed it
up at the church door, to let every

body know that *Polly Meanwell*, the
little ragged girl, had found a large sum
of money, and a fine diamond ring, and
that the owner might have it on describ-
ing the purse and ring.

They lady hearing of this, sent for
Polly and described the purse and ring,
which *Polly* returned to her, who gave
her ten guineas. " And now *Polly*,"
says she, " as I know you are a very
' honest, religious, and good girl, I
' will provifie for you. Go into the
' next room, and strip off your rag-
' ged cloaths, and put on those new
' ones you'll find on the great chair,
' and you shall wait on my daughter
' to the *East Indies*; where, if you
' behave in the same manner you have
' hitherto done, you will become a
' great woman; for God Almighty
' will certainly blefs you."

Some years after this, and when
Polly was grown a woman the lady
set off for the *East-Indies*, and *Polly*
with her. But in their passage, they
were taken by *Angria* the pirate; and
poor *Polly*, being a beautiful girl
was again reduced to great distress
for *Angria* made several attempts on
her virtue, and because she would no

comply with his wicked defires, he put her into a dark prifon, and would not fuffer her miftrefs to fee her. Now this happened at a time when *Kolan-mi-Dolan* a very rich king in *India*, came to vifit his dominions ; for part of which, *Angria* the pirate paid him a tribute ; and fhe having been punifhed on account of her virtue, procured her freedom of *Angria*, and took her with him to his palace of *Itftohan*.

King *Kolan-mi Dolan* intended to make her one of his concubines ; but *Polly* was determined not to be guilty of any thing fo wicked, fhe therefore fell on her knees to him and faid,

" O king! you have done a glorious
" action in delivering me from that
" wicked man *Angria*, for which I
" hope God Almighty will amply re-
" ward you; for he hath promised to
" be a friend to those who defend the
" innocent, and support the helpless.
" Do not therefore, O king, lose the

" blessing of the Almighty, and fully
" your own honour, by depriving me
" of my virtue, which I hold more
" dear than life itself. Ah! why
" should you for a sensual gratifica-
" tion, a momentary pleasure, make me
" miserable for ever? Consider, I be-
" seech you, before whom you stand:
" God Almighty takes notice of your
" actions as well as mine, nor can
" these things be hid from his sight:
" for the darkness is no darkness with
" him; but the night is as clear as
" the day. You and all your hosts
" are but as nothing with respect to
" him. Look in the charnel houses
" of your fathers, where is now their
" power, their pomp, their gran-
" deur? they are now but dust, and
' mingled with the dross of mankind.
" Why then should pride tempt you to
" provoke God, or wickedness prompt

" you to commit a fin, which perhaps
" may be your overthrow ? Kill me
" you may, but you fhall never deprive
" me of my virtue and honour."

Kolan mi Dolan was fo furprifed at
this heroic anfwer, that for a confider-
able time he could make no reply : he
was dumb with amazement, and fix-
ing his eyes on the beloved object, he

resolved in his soul the instability of human grandeur, the majesty of the deity, the dignity of virtue, and the power and persuasive force of kneeling artless innocence. He then raised *Polly* from the ground, and addressed himself to her in these words: " O my divine creature ! " thou art marked out by Providence to " read me the lecture I most wanted, to " teach me to turn my thoughts to their " proper centre, and to search the bottom of my heart. Ambition, pride, " luxury, and revenge had planted " themselves there : but thou hast, by " thy prudence and angelic virtue, ba- " nished them thence. I now see my- " self, and admire and adore thy supe- " rior sense and virtue. Be my compa- ' nion for life, and I will this moment " discharge all my concubines, the crea- " tors of my luxury and folly, and make ' myself for ever happy with thee only."

He then married mifs *Polly* in the moft
folmen manner, according to the cere-
monies of her religion, and built for
her a palace of jafper, the front of which
was overlaid with pure gold, the floor
paved with pearls and diamonds, and the
cielings adorned with the moft curious
paintings of facred hiftory. She had a
large garden richly decorated with the

fineſt grottos, groves, mazey walks, fountains, and purling ſtreams. The turf in it bears continual verdure, the moſt delicious fruits bow down the labouring branches, to ſalute the enchanted eye, and the never-fading flowers pay an eternal tribute to her piety and virtue. Here ſhe every evening recreates herſelf with thoſe ladies of her court who

are most distinguished for their virtue
and good sense; but her mornings are
always spent in hearing the complaints
of her people, and promoting their
happiness. Virtues or vices fly from
the court, and disperse themselves
through a country, in the same manner as the fashions and garbs of dress;
what is sworn by the great will be af-

ected by the meaner fort. Hence it
followed, that the morality and good
principles cultivated at court, by mifs
Polly the Queen, were foon fpread through-
out all the kingdom, and it became fa-
hionable to be virtuous and honeft.
And what was at firft introduced through
afhion, is now maintained through pru-
ence; for as it became unfafhionable to
be wicked, the murders, adulteries, rob-
eries, thefts, &c. with which the na-
ion was continually plagued before, were
now not fo much as heard of, and the
people found, that in confequence of be-
ng VIRTUOUS they became HAPPY.

FINIS.